Puppy In my Pocket

Best Friends

SCHOLASTIC READER 3
700-1500 WORDS

By Sierra Harimann
Illustrated by The Artifact Group

SCHOLASTIC INC.

New York   Toronto   London   Auckland

Sydney   Mexico City   New Delhi   Hong Kong

ISBN 978-0-545-34192-9

Published by Scholastic Inc. SCHOLASTIC and associated logos are trademarks and/or registered trademarks of Scholastic Inc.
Lexile is a registered trademark of MetaMetrics, Inc.

12 11 10 9 8 7 6 5 4 3 2   12 13 14 15 16/0

Designed by Angela Jun
Printed in the U.S.A.   40
First printing, January 2012

It was a rainy day in Puppyville.

Freddy sighed. "I was really looking forward to going to the park," he said sadly. "Staying inside is so boring."

Suddenly Gigi let out a happy bark.

"*Ooh, la la!*" she said. "I just got the most exciting e-mail!"

"What is it?" Sammy asked eagerly.

"My cousin Pierre is coming to visit from Paris," Gigi explained. "He's going to stay at Puppyville Manor all year!"

"I love meeting new puppies," Freddy said. "We can throw him a welcome party!"

"He would love that," Gigi replied. "Pierre is so much fun. I know everyone will like him."

"Who is Pierre?" Fuji asked as she shook out her umbrella.

She and Montana had just returned from the market.

"He's Gigi's cousin," Sammy said. "He's from Paris."

"He's coming to live in Puppyville!" Gigi barked happily.

The puppies started getting ready for Pierre's arrival right away.

Fuji and Freddy hung blue, white, and red streamers, and French flags.

Gigi made *steak frites*, her favorite French dish.
Montana baked dog biscuits shaped like little Eiffel
Towers for dessert.

The next day, the puppies were so excited to meet Pierre.

Finally, the doorbell rang.

"I'll get it!" yelped Gigi as she raced to the door and opened it.

"*Bonjour, Pierre!*" Gigi shouted.

"Welcome to Puppyville Manor!" the other puppies barked.

"Hi, Pierre," Fuji greeted him. "Let me take your bag."
"And I'll take your hat!" Clarissa said.
"Please, have a seat," Spike barked.

"Would you like some *steak frites*?" Freddy asked. "Or how about a dog biscuit?" Montana held out a plate to Pierre.

"What is this?" Pierre asked as he sniffed at the food.

"It's steak," Freddy replied. "Gigi made it for you."

Pierre wrinkled his nose.

"I don't like steak," Pierre said. "I like snails. That's what I eat in France."

"Oh, I'm sorry!" Gigi barked softly. "I didn't know."

Pierre yawned loudly.

"I'm very tired," he said. "I think I'm going to take a nap."

And with that, he curled up and began to snore.

The other puppies didn't know what to do.

No one felt like having a party while the guest of honor was asleep.

So the puppies quietly took down all the decorations.

Pierre slept and slept.

When he finally woke up, it was dark outside.

The other puppies were gone. They were asleep in their beds upstairs.

For a minute, Pierre forgot where he was. The shadows made scary shapes on the wall!

Pierre felt scared and lonely.

After a while, he finally fell asleep again.

The next morning, the puppies ate breakfast together.

"Good morning!" everyone barked at once.

Pierre tried to reply, but it was so loud that no one heard him.

Pierre pushed his oatmeal around, but didn't eat much.

He liked croissants for breakfast.

Pierre sighed. He missed France.

After breakfast, the puppies had places to g
Fuji and Montana went to yoga.
Spike, Freddy, and Clarissa had music class.
And Sammy went to the library.

"Sorry, Pierre!" Gigi said. "I promised Ivy I would go dress shopping with her. Let's do something later, okay?"

"Sure," Pierre said with a shrug. Then he headed outside to take a walk.

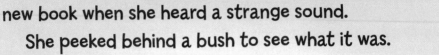

Sammy was on her way home from the library with a
new book when she heard a strange sound.
She peeked behind a bush to see what it was.

It was Pierre! It looked like he had been crying. "What happened, Pierre?" Sammy asked. "Is everything okay?"

Pierre wiped his eyes with his paw.
"I'm homesick," Pierre said. "And I don't think the other puppies like me."

Sammy sat down next to him.

"Well, maybe you were a little unfriendly," Sammy said gently.

"But I didn't mean it!" Pierre barked sadly. "I was just tired. And everything here is different. I'm really sorry. I just want to make some new friends."

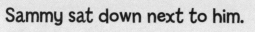

"You already have one new friend — me!" Sammy said. "And I know how you can make a few more. Just be honest. The other puppies will understand."

"Thanks, Sammy," Pierre said. He smiled.

When Sammy and Pierre got back to Puppyville Manor, everyone was home.

"*Bonjour*," Pierre barked. "I'm sorry for not being friendly yesterday. You were all so nice, but I was shy and scared to be meeting so many new puppies. Can we be friends?"

"Of course we can be friends!" said Spike.
The other puppies barked in agreement.
"We're sorry, too," Gigi said. "We should have let you unpack before we had your welcome party."

"That's okay," Pierre said. "It was a nice party. I was just too tired to enjoy it!"

The puppies all laughed.

"Why don't we have another party now?" Freddy suggested.

"Great idea!" Gigi agreed. "Turn up the music and let's dance!"

"I'm not a good dancer," Pierre whispered to Sammy.

"That's okay," Sammy replied. "I'll show you how!"

"Thanks, Sammy." Pierre smiled. "I think we're going to be best friends!"